孩子的模仿力強，吸收力佳，在還沒形成地方口音之前，就讓他學習說英語，可避免**晚一天學，多一天困難**的煩惱！外國語言的學習，有助於智力的開發，及見聞的增長。前教育部次長阮大年說：「早學英語的好處很多。我**小學四年級就開始學英語**以致到了台灣唸中學，我一直名列前茅。」

　　「**學習兒童美語讀本**」1－3冊出版以來，各校老師都認為這套讀本活潑有趣的學習方式，可讓兒童快快樂樂地學會說英語。在各界的鼓勵下，我們配合教育部將**英語列入國小**選修課程的實施，企劃出齊「**學習兒童美語讀本**」全套六冊，使這套教材更趨完備。

對小朋友而言：本套書以日常生活常遇到的狀況為中心，讓小朋友從身邊的事物開始學英文。實用、生動而有創意的教材，小朋友更能自然親近趣味盎然的英語！

對教學者而言：本套書編序完整，教學者易於整理，各頁教材之下，均有教學提示，老師不必多花時間，就可獲得事半功倍的準備效果。此外，每單元均有唱歌、遊戲、美勞等活動，老師能在輕鬆愉快的方式下，順利教學！

對父母親而言：兒童心理學上，「親子教學法」對孩子學習能力的增強，有很大的幫助。本套書在每單元之後，均附有在家學習的方法，提供具體的方法和技巧，可以幫助家長與子女的共同學習！

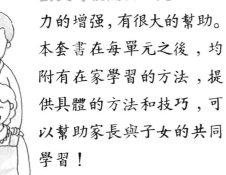

透過這套書，兒童學習英語的過程，必然是輕鬆愉快。而且，由於開始時所引發的興趣，未來的學習將充滿興奮與期待！

本 書 特 色

● 學習語言的基本順序，是 Hearing（聽）、Speaking（說）、Reading（讀）、Writing（寫），本套教材即依此原則編輯。

● 內容背景本土化、國情化，使兒童在熟悉的環境中學習英語，避免像其他原文兒童英語書，與現實生活有出入的弊端。

● 題材趣味化、生活化，學了立即能在日常生活中使用。

● 將英語歌曲、遊戲，具有創意的美勞，與學習英語巧妙地組合在一起，以提高兒童的學習興趣，達到寓教於樂的目的。

● 每單元的教材均有教學指導和提示，容易教學。而且每單元之末均列有目標說明，指導者易於掌握重點。

● 提供在家學習的方法，家長們可親自教導自己的子女學習英語，除加強親子關係外，也達到自然的學習成效。

● 每單元終了，附有考查學習成果的習作，有助於指導者了解學生的吸收力。

● 書末附有總複習，以加深學習印象。另外，在下一冊書的前面也有各種方式的複習，以達到溫故知新的目的。

本套書以六歲兒童到國二學生為對象，是全國唯一與國中英語課程相銜接的美語教材。學完六冊的小朋友，上了國中，既輕鬆又愉快。

CONTENTS

Review 1 > **My Hobby**

Look and read.

My Hobby

Name: John **Grade:** 6 **Date:** 2/24

My hobby is . is interesting. I **like** my stamps with my .

I **began** when I was in the third grade. My gave all his stamps at that time, because he was **so** busy **that** he didn't have time to collect them.

My come from many countries. They **look beautiful**. I **enjoy learning** about different countries this way.

(Note) : Let students practice reading the sentences by replacing pictures with words. Don't let them write down the answers. If they do read very well, let them read this one by one.

Review 2 > Passive Voice & Relative Pronouns

Make sentences.

Susan/make　　Wayne/wash　　Mary's uncle/write　　Tom/paint

Example:　The dress was made by Susan.

The girl is my sister.　　The book is on the desk.　　The cookies are delicious.

I know the boy.　　We will visit the girl.　　This is the car.

Example:　The girl who is playing tennis is my sister.

Review 3 　 A New Model Airplane

Look and read.

Tom : John, what's in your hand?

John : It's the new model airplane **that** my father gave me for my birthday.

Tom : Oh! **How pretty it is**! It is very expensive, **isn't it**?

John : Yes. I **have looked** forward to it for a long time.

Tom : If I **had** a lot of money, I **could buy** one.

John : If I **were** you, I **would save** my money now.

Review 4 > My Best Friend

Read and say.

In the fifth grade I knew a very shy girl. She **never** talked. She **never** played with anyone and she just **watched** us **play** by the window. She had **no** friends. I was sorry for her. Every day I tried to say something to **make** her **happy.** "Your new pencil case **looks pretty.**" "You can have **either** my sandwiches **or** my cookies." "Your voice **sounds sweet**."

She **never** answered a word. But on the last day of school she was waiting at the gate. She put her mouth to my ear and said, "Thank you for everything!" We **have been** good friends ever since.

A NEW SCHOOL YEAR

Mr. Wang :	Hello, everyone. I am Mr. Wang. Welcome to my English class. You have all studied English for the past two years. Do you like English? I am sure you do. Today I'd like you to say something about yourselves to your new friends. Tom, what do you say first when you meet new friends?
Tom :	We say "Hi," "Hello," or some other greeting.
Mr. Wang :	That's good. Anything else?
Mark :	Your name.

Mr. Wang :	Your name. Yes, that's the most important thing. And when you say your name, you must speak slowly and clearly.
Paul :	Your age.
Mr. Wang :	Yes, if you think age is important. Sometimes you don't have to say your age.
Susan :	Something special about yourself.
Mr. Wang :	Yes, you're right. Something special, such as your favorite sport or hobby. That is sure to interest your new friends.
Mary :	How about your family?
Mr. Wang :	Good. Oh, I almost forgot one thing. It's nice to say "thank you" when you finish. Well, who wants to be the first?
Mary :	Can I try first?
Mr. Wang :	Sure. Go ahead!

Hello, everyone! My name is Mary. I live with my family in this city. My father is a doctor. My mother works in a library. Every morning they go to work together by car. I like playing volleyball. I've played volleyball for two years. Thank you!

Hi! How are you? My name is Mark. I have several hobbies. One of them is listening to music. Michael Jackson is my favorite singer. I also like Natural Science very much. I'm going to be a pilot when I grow up. Thank you.

Hello, Mr. Wang. I am Paul. I am twelve years old. I like English and Science very much. I like playing sports, too. One of my favorite sports is baseball. I always play baseball with my classmates after class. Thank you.

 1-1 LET'S PRACTICE

Look and write.

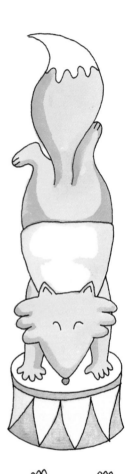

Something about myself

Put your photo here.

Name: _____

Age: _____

Birthday: _____

Elementary School: _____

Grade: _____

Hobbies: _____ _____

Favorite sport: _____

Favorite music: _____

Favorite TV program: _____

Favorite food: _____

Favorite subject: _____ _____

Least favorite subject: _____

(Note) : Teach the students to fill in the table. Then encourage them to introduce themselves using this format.

 **SING A SONG**

Do Your Ears Hang Low?

Do your ears hang low? Do they wob-ble to and fro?

Can you tie 'em in a knot? Can you tie 'em in a bow?

Can you throw 'em o'er your shoul-der like a

con-tin-en-tal sol-dier? Do your ears hang low?

EXERCISE

Hello. How are you? My name is _____ . I am _____ years old. My birthday is on _____ _____ . I go to _____ Elementary School. I'm in the _____ grade. I have several hobbies. One of them is _____ . My favorite sport is _____ . My favorite TV program is _____ . I like to eat _____ (**food**) very much.

_____ (**subject**) is my favorite school subject. I am going to be a (an) _____ when I grow up. Thank you.

(Note)： Let students practice the paragraph until everyone has memorized it. Have students close their books, then choose a volunteer to introduce himself.

■ **本單元目標**：使學生做簡單明確的自我介紹，必須包含基本個人資料，能很清晰地使別人認識自己。

■ **在家學習的方法**：家長可讓孩子們利用 Exercise 的範例來替 Susan、Tom、Helen 等做自我介紹。平常家中有客人來訪時，也不妨讓孩子用英文做自我介紹。

2 A BIRTHDAY PRESENT

Bill Green had a girlfriend. He loved her very much. She had deep blue eyes.

"I'm going to marry her," he said to his friends. But one day a car hit her, and she died.

"I'm not going to marry anyone," he said to himself. Every day he worked at his store from nine to six.

Five years passed. One day a little girl came into Bill's store. Her eyes were deep blue.

"Hello," said the girl. "I want that dress in the window."

"O.K.," said Bill. "Are you going to buy it for your mother?"

"No," said the girl. "My mother died last year. I'm going to give it to my big sister. Tomorrow is her birthday."

The girl took all the coins out of her pocket.

"This is all my money," she said. "Two dollars and seventy-five cents."

The dress was thirty-nine dollars. But the girl didn't see the price.

"Is that enough?" asked the girl.

"Well... yes, of course it's all right," said Bill. The girl looked very happy.

About six o'clock the next day, a young woman came in. She had large blue eyes.

She showed a dress to Bill and said, "My little sister Mary bought this dress here. How did she pay for it? Perhaps she had only a dollar or two."

"She paid all her money," said Bill. "She is a kind girl. That was enough for me."

A few days later, Mary and her sister Helen invited Bill to dinner. Helen looked very beautiful in her new dress. Bill had a happy evening for the first time in five years.

The next year on her birthday, Mary got a wonderful present—a new big brother. On that day her sister and Bill married, and he became a good brother to Mary.

Questions:

1. **Did Bill work at his store every day?**

2. **Did Mary have blue eyes or brown eyes?**

3. **How much did the girl pay for the dress?**

4. **Why did Bill go to Mary's home?**

2-1 **LET'S PRACTICE**

(1) Look and say.

Example: Helen **is going to** call Mark.

(2) Choose the correct words.

Words for you: funny animals came pictures zoo
                  lunch joined stood took was

Yesterday Tom and I went to the (   ).

I took some (   ) of Tom with different kinds of

(   ). When we had (   ) on the grass, some girl students

(   ) us. I (   ) a picture of them with Tom.

But when it (   ) out, Tom (   ) surprised to find that

a monkey (   ) between the girls and him.

He looks like a father monkey and this makes this photo

look (   ).

(Note) : This unit reviews the "be going to" sentence pattern and the past tense.

thirteen

 **LEARN THE RHYME**

Mother Goose

Christmas is coming,
  The geese are getting fat;
Please put a penny
  In the old man's hat.

If you haven't got a penny,
  A smile will do.
If you haven't got a smile,
  God bless you.

I love little Kitty,
  Her coat is so warm;
And if I don't hurt her,
  She'll do me no harm.

So I'll not pull her tail,
  Nor drive her away,
But Kitty and I
  Very gently will play.

I'll sit by the fire,
  And give her some food,
And Kitty will love me
  Because I am good.

2-③ EXERCISE

Fill in the blanks.

A

1. He _____ the car last Sunday. (wash)
2. They _____ to the library last week. (go)
3. _____ Jane and Nancy busy yesterday? (are)
4. Tom _____ English three years ago. (study)
5. My father _____ me a pretty dog last year. (give)
6. Mr. Smith _____ cats when he was young. (like)
7. Jane and Mary _____ Taipei two years ago. (visit)
8. There _____ a library in this city last year. (is)
9. His uncle _____ two dogs in his house last year. (has)
10. _____ English difficult for you when you were a child? (is)
11. Our class _____ at 8:30 last Wednesday. (begin)
12. _____ your mother _____ a book for you? (buy)

B

1. I _____ write a letter this evening.
2. Ben _____ _____ free tomorrow.
3. I am _____ to study Math.
4. _____ Tom get up at seven tomorrow?
5. Helen _____ _____ to listen to the radio after dinner.

■ 本單元目標：這課主要是複習be going to的句型及動詞過去式的用法。
■ 在家學習的方法：家長可以逐段講解課文，利用溫馨有趣的故事培養孩子閱讀文章的耐心，再一面點出本課的複習重點。

3 ASKING THE WAY

1 An American gentleman speaks to Mark.

Gentleman:	Excuse me. Can you help me?
Mark :	Yes, I can.
Gentleman:	Where is the department store? I want a camera.
Mark :	It's not so far from here. Let's walk together.

Mark :	The department store is on this street.
Gentleman:	Oh, is it? I'm a stranger here.
Mark :	Where are you from?
Gentleman:	I'm from San Francisco. This is my first visit to Taiwan.
Mark :	Are you here on a pleasure trip?
Gentleman:	Yes, I am.

Mark :	Do you see that big building over there?
Gentleman:	Well, there are two big buildings. Which is the department store?

Mark :	The new building.
Gentleman:	Thank you very much.
Mark :	You're welcome.

② A: Excuse me, but could you
    tell me the way to the
    nearest stop?
   B: All right. Just keep going,
    and turn to the right at the
    second corner. You will
    find the bus stop in front
    of a bank.
   A: Thank you very much.
   B: You are welcome.

③ A: Does this bus go to the
    City Park?
   B: No, it doesn't. You should
    take Number 5 over there.
   A: How long does it take to
    get to the City Park?
   B: Well, it takes about 20
    minutes.
   A: Thank you very much.
   B: You are welcome.

④ A: Excuse me. How do I get to
    the zoo?
   B: It's too far to walk. You'll
    have to take the bus.
   A: Which bus do I take?
   B: Take Number 1 and get off
    at the City Zoo.
   A: Thank you.

3-1 LET'S PRACTICE

1

2

(Note)： Let students work in pairs and practice asking the way. Use these two maps as guides.

SING A SONG

OH, SUSANNA !

1. I– come from　A - la - ba - ma with　my ban- jo　on my
2. It– rained all　day the night I left　The weath- er was so

knee,　I'm–going to Louis -i- a-na,　My　Su- san-na for　to　see.
dry,　The– sun　so hot　I froze my-self, Su- san- na don't you cry.

Oh,　Su - san-na!　Oh,　don't you cry for　me,　For　I

come from　A - la - ba - ma with　my ban- jo　on　my　knee.

3. I had a dream the other night,
   When everything was still.
   I thought I saw Susanna
   A-coming down the hill.

4. The buckwheat cake was in her mouth,
   A tear was in her eye,
   Says I, "I'm coming from the South."
   Susanna, don't you cry.

 **EXERCISE**

A Multiple choice.

1. There are (some, any, much) eggs in the basket.
2. We have (few, little, many) rain in winter.
3. Mr. Smith is (very, many, much) taller than Bill.
4. I have (much, little, a lot of) books in my room.
5. There is (a few, a little, few) sugar in the cup.

B Make sentences.

1. (usually)

    _____

2. (often)

    _____

3. (never)

    _____

4. (always)

    _____

5. (ever)

    _____

6. (sometimes)

    _____

■本單元目標:讓小朋友練習用英文問路及爲別人指路,並複習以前教過的「數量形容詞」和「頻率副詞」。

■在家學習的方法:家長可利用課文中的對話和孩子做角色扮演的活動。此外在做習題之前,可先爲孩子們複習「數量形容詞」和「頻率副詞」的規則,加深印象。

SUSAN'S PEN PAL

(date)

Dear Steve,

I got your name from our English teacher.

My name is Susan. I live in Taiwan. I am in the sixth grade. I am a member of the English club. English is my favorite subject.

We have a lot of homework every day. My mother always says, "You have to study very hard while you are a student."

Susan Chen
NO. 5 Alley 30 Tung H wa St.
Taipei, Taiwan
R. O. C

Mr. Steve Smith
3232 First Street
New York NY 10021
U. S. A

VIA AIR MAIL

Next I will tell you about my family. There are four people in my family—my father, my mother, my brother and me.

My father works in Taipei. My mother is a school teacher. My brother is in elementary school. He likes to watch TV when he has no homework.

Can you understand my English? I would like to know a lot about your family and school life. Please write me soon.

Your friend,

Susan Chen

(date)

Dear Susan,

Thank you for your wonderful letter.

My father is a doctor. My mother is a nurse. My sister is in high school.

I will tell you about my school life. In America most schools begin in September and end in May. We don't have to go to school in June, July and August.

Last summer my family and I spent one month near a lake in the mountains.

Last week we had a test on math. I didn't do very well on the test. I am not good at math. Are you good at math?

I can understand your English very well. When you have any questions about English, please write and ask me. I will answer them.

Please say hello to your family. Goodbye for now.

Your pen pal,

Steve Smith

(Note) : Teach students how to write an English letter. Pay attention to the correct form of an English letter.

LET'S PRACTICE

Look and write.

 1 You will be Joseph Lee. Write a letter to your new friend Lisa in Los Angeles.

Age : 12
Birthday : March 10
Family : my parents, 2 brothers and me

Father's Job : teacher
Mother's Job : nurse
Personality : outgoing
Hobby : swimming and singing

2 **Now you will be Lisa Jones. Answer a letter from your new friend Joseph in Taiwan.**

_____

_____

_____

_____

_____

_____

_____

_____

_____

_____

Age : 12
Birthday : Dec. 22
Family : my parents and me
Father's Job : doctor
Mother's Job: housewife
Personality : shy
Hobby : collecting stamps

4-2 PLAY A GAME

A secret message.

Nancy received a letter from Tom. She opened the letter. There weren't any words on it. There were only numbers. Nancy showed the message to John. But he didn't understand it. It didn't mean anything to him. Nancy went to her desk, she wrote something on a piece of paper. It was the alphabet. Nancy could understand the message. How about you ?

13-12+24　6+3+9+1+1

4+1-4+17　14-13+13-11+22

14+1+8　25-10+6　3-2+13　10+5-6+5　13+12

3+12-2+3+5-1-15+13　3+9+9-19

20-5-2

A	B	C	D	E	F	G
H	I	J	K	L	M	N
O	P	Q	R	S	T	U
V	W	X	Y	Z		

4-3 EXERCISE

Fill in the blanks.

A

1. You are _____ English now. (study)
2. I was _____ to the radio then. (listen)
3. Your mother is _____ the room now. (clean)
4. Bill and Mike were _____ in the park then. (run)
5. The dog is _____ under the tree. (sleep)
6. They are _____ television in the room. (watch)
7. Father is _____ a newspaper now. (read)
8. Mary was _____ a doll then. (make)
9. Jane's brother is _____ the car. (wash)

B

1. Do you know that man? ⇨ Yes, I know _____ .
2. Did his father meet my brothers yesterday?
   ⇨ No, he didn't meet _____ .
3. Is that Mary's doll? ⇨ Yes, It is_____ .
4. This car is _____ . (you)
5. The bicycle in front of the store is _____ . (I)
6. Mr. Brown gave _____ some books. (Mary and I)
7. Jane played tennis with _____ yesterday. (I)
8. Whose bicycle is this? ⇨ It is _____ . (they)

■ 本單元目標：教小朋友寫一封英文信，並複習「進行式」及「代名詞」的用法。
■ 在家學習的方法：家長可從身邊的事物開始，教孩子寫信，如介紹自己、家人、同學等。平常宜多鼓勵孩子寫信和外國小孩作筆友。

I AM A DOG

I am a dog. I am loved by my master and his family. I am very happy.

My master is forty-one years old. I am ten years old. But in human years I am as old as my master.

My master's wife is as old as my master. But she looks young. She is very busy. She often invites her friends to the house. She is the busiest housewife in the world.

My master's son goes to high school. He is very tall. He is taller than his parents.

The boy says to his parents, "I'm going to the library. I'll be back about eight." But really he sometimes goes out with his girlfriend.

The other day my master called all the family together. He showed them pictures of two dogs, and said, "We'll find a bride for our dog. Which is better, this one or that one?"

After a long time they decided. But I really wanted to say, "Why don't you ask me? I have a right to say something about this."

Do you remember these?

Group 1	old	older	oldest
	tall	taller	tallest
	young	younger	youngest

Group 2	wise	wiser	wisest
	free	freer	freest
	large	larger	largest

Group 3	big	bigger	biggest
	hot	hotter	hottest
	thin	thinner	thinnest

Group 4	angry	angrier	angriest
	early	earlier	earliest
	easy	easier	easiest
	happy	happier	happiest

Group 5	beautiful	more beautiful	most beautiful
	expensive	more expensive	most expensive
	interesting	more interesting	most interesting
	difficult	more difficult	most difficult

Group 6	good	better	best
	bad	worse	worst
	{ many	more	most
	much		

5-1 LET'S PRACTICE

Mr. Mouse : You've grown up now.

Mrs. Mouse: You need a good husband.

Daughter : What about Oliver ?

Mrs. Mouse: Oh, no. Oliver is too poor.

Mr. Mouse : You should marry the strongest man in the world.

Mrs. Mouse: But who could that be ?

Mr. Mouse : I know ! Mr. Sun ! Mr. Sun, please come out !

Characters
Mr. Mouse
Mrs. Mouse
Daughter Mouse
Oliver Mouse
Sun
Cloud
Wind
Wall

(Mr. Sun comes out.)

Mr. Sun : Hello, Mr. and Mrs. Mouse. What can I do for you ?

Mrs. Mouse: We're looking for a husband for our daughter.

Mr. Mouse : We want the strongest man in the world.

Mr. Sun : I am not the strongest. There is someone even stronger than I.

Mrs. Mouse: Who is he ?

Mr. Sun : It is Mr. Cloud. When he covers me, I can't shine anymore.

Mr. Mouse : Oh, I see.

Mrs. Mouse: Thanks anyway, Mr. Sun !

Mr. Sun : Goodbye !

Mr. Mouse :   Mr. Cloud, please come out !

(Mr. Cloud comes out.)

Mr. Cloud :   Hello, Mr. and Mrs. Mouse. What can I do for you ?

Mrs. Mouse: We're looking for a husband for our daughter.

Mr. Mouse :   We want the strongest man in the world.

Mr. Cloud :   I am not the strongest. There is someone even stronger than I.

Mrs. Mouse: Who is he ?

Mr. Cloud :   It is Mr. Wind. He can blow me away.

Mr. Mouse :   Oh, I see.

Mrs. Mouse: Thanks anyway, Mr. Cloud !

Mr. Cloud :   Goodbye !

Mr. Mouse :   Mr. Wind, please come out !

(Mr. Wind comes out.)

Mr. Wind :   Hello, Mr. and Mrs. Mouse. What can I do for you?

Mrs. Mouse: We're looking for a husband for our daughter.

Mr. Mouse :   We want the strongest man in the world.

Mr. Wind :   I am not the strongest. There is someone even stronger than I.

Mrs. Mouse: Who is he?

Mr. Wind :   It is Mr. Wall. No matter how hard I try, I cannot blow him down.

Mr. Mouse :   Oh, I see.

Mrs. Mouse: Thanks anyway, Mr. Wind!

Mr. Wind :   Goodbye!

Mr. Mouse :   Mr. Wall, please come out!

(Mr. Wall comes out.)

Mr. Wall :   Hello, Mr. and Mrs. Mouse. What can I do for you?

Mrs. Mouse: We're looking for a husband for our daughter.

Mr. Mouse :   We want the strongest man in the world.

Mr. Wall :   I am not the strongest. There is someone even stronger than I.

Mrs. Mouse:　Who is he ?

Mr. Wall :　Shh ! Here he comes !

(Everyone acts frightened. Oliver Mouse comes out.)

Oliver :　Hello, Mr. and Mrs. Mouse.

Mrs. Mouse:　Oliver ?

Mr. Wall :　That's him ! That mouse is the strongest. His teeth frighten me !

Mr. Mouse :　Then he must be the strongest.

Daughter :　Oliver !

Oliver :　I brought you some flowers, dear.

Mr. Mouse :　Oliver, we'd like you to marry our daughter.

Oliver :　I'd love to.

(The sun, cloud, and wall come out.)

All :　Yea ! Congratulations !

Daughter and Oliver :　Thank you ! Thank you !

~ THE END ~

(Note) : Let students practice reading this dialogue and perform it as a play.

PLAY A GAME

Note : The teacher divides the class into teams and writes the words in the right column on the board, choosing one at a time. The students must guess what is special about each thing. Each team wins one point for a right answer. The teacher stops the game after 10 to 15 minutes.

the highest mountain in Taiwan ------------------------- Mt. Jade
the most famous singer in the U.S.A. ------------------ Michael Jackson
the most beautiful place in the city --------------------- the City Park
the biggest animal in the world ------------------------- the whale
etc.

5-3 EXERCISE

A Fill in the blanks.

1. Jane is _____ than Mary. (**tall**)
2. My father is as _____ as Mr. Smith. (**old**)
3. I got up _____ than Bill. (**early**)
4. August is the _____ month in Taiwan. (**hot**)
5. Which is _____ , Taipei or Tainan? (**large**)
6. Mike can run _____ of all the boys. (**fast**)
7. Your bicycle is _____ than mine. (**good**)
8. The pen is _____ _____ than the pencil.
   (**expensive**)
9. The city is _____ than the countryside. (**noisy**)
10. Sue is the _____ girl in our class. (**quiet**)

B Read and answer.

Bill is ten years old. Tom is thirteen years old. Mark is fifteen years old. Tom can run faster than Bill. Mark can run fastest of the three.

1. Who is older, Tom or Mark ?
2. Who is younger, Mark or Bill ?
3. Who is the oldest of the three ?
4. Who can run faster, Tom or Bill ?
5. Who can run fastest of the three ?

■ **本單元目標**：複習「比較級」和「最高級」的用法，老師可利用本單元的表格教同學們將形容詞改為比較級和最高級的規則。

■ **在家學習的方法**：家長可和孩子們一起演戲，並指出其中「比較級」和「最高級」的用法。

6 ♠ SUSAN WENT TO NEW YORK

Susan's pen pal Steve Smith invited her to New York. She is now on the plane. She is very happy.

"We will take off in a few minutes. Please fasten your seat belt. Our flight to New York will take twelve and a half hours. Please enjoy your flight. Thank you."

Susan :	Excuse me. What time is it in New York Now?
Stewardess:	It's 8:12 in the morning.
Susan :	Thank you.
Stewardess:	You are welcome.
Susan :	We will arrive in New York on time, won't we?
Stewardess:	Yes, we will. We left Taipei at noon. We'll arrive in New York at 11:30 a.m. on the same day.
Susan :	Oh, that's strange!

Officer :   Can I see your passport, please ?

Susan :   Yes, here it is.

Officer :   How long will you stay in the United States?

Susan :   For two weeks.

Officer :   All right. You are a student, aren't you?

Susan :   Yes.

Officer :   Have a nice holiday.

Susan :   Hi, Steve ! Nice to see you.

Steve :   Hi, Susan. How was your flight ?

Susan :   It was wonderful. I saw many tall buildings from the plane. They looked great.

Steve :   That's nice. My dad will be here soon. He is calling my mom.

Susan :   Your house is near the airport, isn't it ?

Steve :   No. It takes about an hour by car.

 **6-1 LET'S PRACTICE**

Read and say.

I want to be a scientist.
Studying science is very interesting.

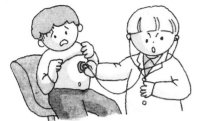

I want to be a doctor.
Doctors help sick people get well.

I want to be a mailman.
I enjoy bringing people good news.

I want to be a teacher.
It's not easy to become a good teacher, but I'll do my best.

What do you want to be?

nurse	farmer	cook
singer	police officer	teacher
taxi driver	clerk	doctor
waiter	fireman	mailman
secretary	businessman	scientist

Note : Help students choose an occupation, then let students prepare themselves for a short speech.

SING A SONG

ROW, ROW, ROW YOUR BOAT

Row, row, row your boat

Gen - tly down the stream, ——

Mer - ri - ly, mer - ri - ly, mer - ri - ly, mer - ri - ly,

Life is but a dream. ——

EXERCISE

Fill in the blanks.

A

1. Those are your watches, <u>aren't</u> <u>they</u>?
2. Jane is an American girl, _____ _____?
3. The man won't come here again, _____ _____?
4. Jim has finished reading the book, _____ _____?
5. Tom's father didn't go to London last year, _____ _____?
6. Helen studies music very hard, _____ _____?
7. You can swim very well, _____ _____?
8. Mary was busy yesterday, _____ _____?

B

1. I finished _____ the dishes. (wash)
2. _____ a walk in the morning is good for us. (take)
3. Did you enjoy _____ cards with your friends? (play)
4. _____ _____ is my hobby. (collect stamps)
5. When I came into the room, Tom stopped _____ television. (watch)

■ 本單元目標：複習「附加問句」及「動名詞」的用法。此外訓練同學們上台用英語做小小演說。
■ 在家學習的方法：家長可與第五冊的第4課和第5課搭配，讓孩子加深印象。

 7 KEEPING A DIARY

Mary's Diary

Sat. Apr. 4.

Dad took John and me to the lake. He likes to fish there. The road leads through the green fields to the lake. It was hot but it was a pleasant ride. John and I swam and Dad fished.

We came home at seven. We were a little tired. Have I finished everything for today? Oh, no. I haven't! I forgot to water the flowers. I'll water them early tomorrow morning.

Helen's Diary

Sun. May 1. Rainy

I got up at seven. It was raining. The color of the sky was gray. We haven't seen the sun for more than a week. We are now in the rainy season.

It stopped raining before noon, but soon it began to fall again. I went to see a movie. Walking in the rain was not pleasant. But the movie was quite interesting.

Peter's Diary

Thurs. March 27.

It has gotten a little cooler. I'll be a junior high school student soon. The school is close to my house.

Getting into a new life is a little exciting.

This afternoon I was invited to Tom's house. Today was his birthday. We had a very good time. On my way home, I bought some notebooks at the bookstore. I met Mark there. I don't know what he bought.

Tom's Diary

Monday, May 7.

Every morning I take Baby for a walk. There is a park near my house. I often go there. I meet Mr. Wang in the park. He takes his dog Lucky with him. He says to me, "Baby is a nice dog." Baby is big and strong. But he has a strange habit. He often hides my mother's shoes. My mother gets angry. We all laugh and say, "He likes you."

7-1 LET'S PRACTICE

Keep your own diary.

(date) _____

_____

_____

_____

_____

_____

_____

_____

_____

_____

_____

_____

_____

Note : Teach students to keep their own diary. If it is a little difficult for them, set up some events for them.

 **PLAY A GAME**

An IQ test.

(1) Can you cut up these apples so that each child has an equal amount?

(2) How many verbs can you find?

b	e	g	i	n	u	o	p	e	n
a	u	o	h	r	n	s	a	j	m
c	s	y	k	g	d	v	c	k	v
e	w	r	i	t	e	x	f	i	o
h	i	b	l	w	r	t	s	a	y
j	m	d	n	a	s	i	n	g	r
o	j	r	p	l	t	e	a	c	h
y	u	f	e	k	a	k	n	o	w
n	m	e	a	a	n	w	g	m	p
e	p	u	t	q	d	y	r	e	n

 **Answers:**

(1) All you have to do is cut each apple into fours and give three pieces to each child.

(2) begin, open, write, say, sing, teach, know, put, enjoy, swim, jump, go, eat, walk, understand, come, buy, get, read, sleep, visit

7-3 EXERCISE

Change the sentences into passive voice.

1. The man opened the door.

   _____

2. Tom made these boxes yesterday.

   _____

3. Father called this dog Lucky.

   _____

4. We can see this flower all over the world.

   _____

5. My uncle gave me a camera.

   _____

6. They speak English in this country.

   _____

7. My brother broke the window yesterday.

   _____

8. Tom's uncle caught the lion in Africa.

   _____

9. He takes the dog to the park every morning.

   _____

10. They built a tall building near the river.

   _____

■ **本單元目標**：複習「被動式」be＋p.p. 的句型及訓練同學們寫日記的習慣。
■ **在家學習的方法**：家長可唸出主動的句子，讓孩子口頭練習，改爲被動式，此外可規定孩子每天用英文寫日記，訓練寫作能力。

8 TWO SHORT STORIES

One afternoon a young man and his girlfriend were riding a horse across his farm. There was not a cloud in the sky. The birds were singing in the trees. A cow and her baby were rubbing noses.

The man said, "Look at those cows. I'd like to do the same thing. We have known each other for a month now."

"Well...why not?" said the girl. "It's your cow, isn't it?"

A rich woman invited a famous singer to sing at her dinner party. The singer was surprised and a little angry when she asked him to eat with the cooks, but he said nothing. Later the rich woman called him. "We're ready," she said.

"I have already sung," replied the singer. "I sang for the people I had dinner with."

 **LET'S PRACTICE**

Look and say.

A: How long have you played the piano?
B: I have played the piano for three years.

**study English/
three years**

**play tennis/
two years**

**watch TV/
three hours**

**live in this city/
twelve years**

**wait for the bus/
forty-five minutes**

**collect stamps/
one month**

 **SING A SONG**

Old Black Joe

Gone are the days   when my   heart was young and gay,

Gone are my friends from the   cot - ton   fields a - way,

Gone   from the earth to a   bet-ter land   I know,   I

hear   their gen - tle voic - es call - ing   "Old   Black   Joe."

I'm com-ing, I'm com-ing,   for my   head is bend-ing low: I

hear those gen-tle   voic-es call-ing "Old Black   Joe."

8-3 EXERCISE

Fill in the blanks.

1. Bill has just _____ the door. (**open**)

2. Jane has already _____ her homework. (**finish**)

3. They haven't _____ lunch yet. (**eat**)

4. Has your father _____ the book? (**read**)

5. Tom has _____ the box. (**make**)

6. Mark hasn't_____ his homework yet. (**do**)

7. I _____ already _____ my room. (**clean**)

8. Tom's mother_____ just_____ breakfast. (**cook**)

9. She has _____ us an interesting story. (**tell**)

10. My uncle _____ _____ English for two years. (**study**)

11. I have _____ Mr. Smith for three years. (**know**)

12. Peter has _____ to New York. (**go**)

13. My sister has never _____ a car before. (**drive**)

14. I've never _____ of it. (**hear**)

■ **本單元目標**：本課主要在複習「現在完成式」have(has)＋p.p.的句型。老師可拿出第五冊中的動詞三態變化表，讓同學們一個個背誦。
■ **在家學習的方法**：家長可先將第五冊後面所附的動詞三態變化表拿出，讓孩子複習一遍。熟練之後，再上本單元。

A PRESENT FOR YOU

One dollar and eighty-seven cents. That was all. Della counted it again. $1.87.

She stood up and looked out of the window. She saw a gray cat that had large gray eyes. It was walking on the gray wall. Everything looked gray.

The next day was Christmas Day. Della wanted to get a present for Jim, but she did not have enough money.

"Is there anything that I can sell?" she said to herself.

Then she stood before the glass and looked at her rich hair for a long time.

Della went to a shop near her house. In the shop she saw a woman who was sitting behind the counter.

"Will you buy my hair?" asked Della.

"I buy hair," said the woman. "Take off your hat."

Della took it off.

"Twenty dollars," said the woman.

Della ran to a shop and bought a watch chain. It was twenty-one dollars.

"Jim's gold watch will look nice on this chain," she thought.

It became dark. Soon Jim came back. He opened the door, and looked at his wife.

"Don't look at me that way, Jim," cried Della. "Say 'Merry Christmas.' I've got something that you've wanted for a long time."

"I've got this for you," said Jim. He put something on the table. It was a small box. Della opened it. She looked at the pretty combs which were in it.

"Oh, Jim !" cried Della.

Both of them were silent for a while. At last Della looked up and smiled.

"My hair grows fast," she said. "Well, I have a present for you, too."

Della took out the watch chain. It was shining beautifully.

"You like it, don't you? You'll have to look at the time a hundred times a day now."

"Della," said Jim. "I've sold the watch. I sold it to get your combs."

LET'S PRACTICE

Look and choose.

	Everything is going well.		Come here.
	I'm full up to here.		Oh! I remember.
	Good luck; I hope it works out.		Me?
	I don't know.		Oh, I forgot!
			Wait a second.

LEARN A RHYME

Teddy Bear

Teddy bear, teddy bear,
Turn around.
Teddy bear, teddy bear,
Touch the ground.
Teddy bear, teddy bear,
Show your shoe.
Teddy bear, teddy bear,
Show what you can do.
Teddy bear, teddy bear,
Go upstairs.
Teddy bear, teddy bear,
Say your prayers.
Teddy bear, teddy bear,
Turn off the light.
Teddy bear, teddy bear,
Say good night.

EXERCISE

A. Fill in the blanks.

1. The girl _____ is writing a letter is my sister.
2. Do you know the students _____ are running in the park?
3. I can't do the homework _____ was given to us yesterday.
4. The blind man and his dog _____ are crossing the street live next to us.
5. The cookies _____ were made by Helen are delicious.

B. Make sentences.

1. Look at the boy. He is swimming in the pool.

   _____

2. This is a car. It was made in Taiwan.

   _____

3. Jack is my friend. He lives in Canada.

   _____

4. I know a boy. He can draw pictures very well.

   _____

■本單元目標：複習「關係代名詞」which、that、who的用法。
■在家學習的方法：家長可讓孩子將課文背下來，並像說故事一般地說給父母、家人聽。除了注重發音外，也可幫助他們學習重要的文法句型。

10 THE LAST LEAF (I)

New York is a wonderful city with many interesting places. Sue and Jenny were young women who were studying art there. Both of them came from different towns to the city. They wanted to become artists. They met in New York in May, and became good friends. Because they were very poor, they lived together in an apartment. In November many people caught bad colds. Jenny was among them.

Sue called a doctor for Jenny. He said to Sue, "Your friend has very little chance to get well again. She doesn't want to live. But she must want to live. She will get better only if she has a strong will to live. Please tell that to her."

Jenny was still in bed, and was looking through the window at the next house. There was a vine on the wall. The leaves were falling faster and faster. Soon almost a hundred had fallen.

"There are only five now," said Jenny.

"Five what?" asked Sue.

"Leaves on that vine. When the last leaf falls, I must go, too," said Jenny.

"Don't say that. Close your eyes. Go to sleep. You'll get well again," Sue said.

Behrman was a poor artist who was over sixty years old. He was Sue and Jenny's neighbor. He always said, "Some day I'll paint a great picture." But he never did.

He was a kind old man. He always took care of Sue and Jenny. He liked the two girls.

Sue went to Mr. Behrman to talk about Jenny. He said to Sue, "Jenny will be better soon. People don't die because leaves fall." Mr. Behrman's words made Sue feel a little better.

They looked out of the window at the leaves. The wind was blowing hard. A cold rain began to fall.

10-1 LET'S PRACTICE

A Answer the questions.

1. Where did Sue and Jenny live ?
2. What was Jenny looking at ?
3. What did Mr. Behrman always say ?
4. Does New York have many interesting places ?
5. When did Sue and Jenny meet ?
6. When did many people catch bad colds ?
7. Who called a doctor ?
8. Was Mr. Behrman a young artist ?

B Suppose you are a friend of Jenny's. Write something to cheer her up.

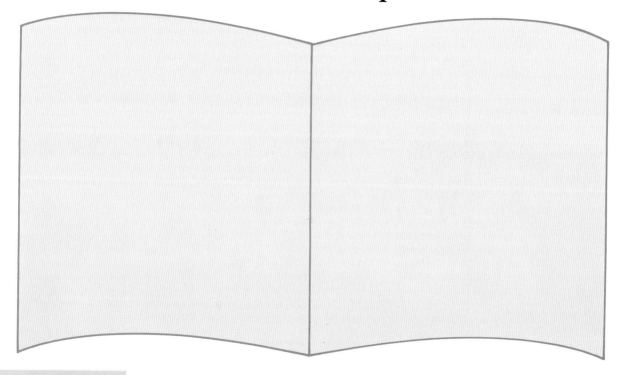

10-2 PERFORM A PLAY

Tom Has to Work on Saturday (I)

(Tom is eating jam in the kitchen. Aunt Polly comes in.)

Tom : The jam really tastes good.

Aunt Polly : What are you doing here, Tom?

Tom : Oh, I'm just going to wash the dishes.

Aunt Polly : Wash your face first. Look at your nose and mouth. You look like a dirty child.

Tom : I can't look at my mouth.

Aunt Polly : Look at your hands then.

Tom : Aunt Polly, I was very hungry, because I....

Aunt Polly : Because you went swimming. You weren't in school today. What a bad boy! You must work tomorrow.

Tom : Oh! On Saturday?

Characters

Tom
Aunt Polly
Ben, Tom's friend
John, Tom's friend
Bob, Tom's friend
Bill, Tom's friend

Note : Let students work in pairs and perform this conversation.

(It is a warm Saturday morning. Tom is painting the fence around the yard. Ben is watching him.)

Ben :　Ha ! Ha ! Today is Saturday, but you have to work, Tom. Shall I help you ?

Tom :　No, thank you. This isn't work. It's fun, and it's very difficult. You can't do it.

Ben :　Yes, I can. It's easy.

Tom :　Oh, no ! You can't.

Ben :　But I want to try. Please. I'll give you my apple. Look !

Tom :　That's a big apple ! All right. You can paint just a little.

EXERCISE

Answer the questions.

1. **How does Mary look ?**
2. **What does the big cloud look like ?**
3. **How does Nancy feel ?**
4. **How does the music sound ?**
5. **How does the cookie taste ?**
6. **How does the flower smell ?**
7. **How does the story sound ?**
8. **What does the cake taste like ?**

■本單元目標：複習 look、feel、taste、sound 加形容詞及 look like、feel like、taste like、sound like 加名詞的句型。

■在家學習的方法：除了課文中的練習之外，可讓孩子利用本課的句型來造句，描寫家中的事物或同學、朋友等。

11 THE LAST LEAF (II)

The next morning Sue and Jenny looked out of the window.

Only one leaf was still there.

Jenny looked tired and said, "That is the last leaf. It will fall today, and I shall die."

In the evening the last leaf was still there. Then, it started raining and blowing again.

The next day the last leaf was still there.

Jenny looked at it for a long time. She looked happier and stronger. Then she said, "What a bad girl I was, Sue. I wanted to die. It was wrong. I've learned from that leaf that it's bad to want to die. Now I want to get well and paint pictures again. Give me some soup, please."

The doctor came in the afternoon. "Your friend is getting better. She will get well before long, if you look after her carefully," he said to Sue. "Now there is another sick person in this building. He's old and weak. He will probably die."

The next morning the doctor told Sue, "Jenny is safe now. If she eats enough food, she will be all right."

In the afternoon Sue came to Jenny and said, "Mr. Behrman died today. He was ill for only two days. When someone went into his room on the morning of the first day, Mr. Behrman was lying there. His shoes and clothes were all wet and as cold as ice. He went out in the rain the night before last and caught a very bad cold."

"Look out of the window at the last leaf on the wall," said Sue. "It looks like a real leaf, doesn't it?"

"A real leaf?"

"It's Behrman's greatest picture. He painted it there on that stormy night after the last leaf fell."

 # 11-1 LET'S PRACTICE

Answer the questions.

1. What did Jenny say when she looked out of the window?
2. What did Jenny say after she looked at the last leaf for a long time?
3. What did Mr. Behrman do in the rain?
4. Why did Mr. Behrman die?
5. What did Jenny learn from the last leaf?
6. How long was Behrman ill?
7. When did Behrman paint the last leaf?
8. What do you think of this story? Write it down in your diary.

date _____

 **11-2 PLAY A GAME**

Tom Has to Work on Saturday (II)

(Tom sits under a tree and begins to eat the apple. Some other boys come along. Everyone wants to paint.)

Tom :　All right, everyone, but you have to give me something to make me happy. What will you give me?

John :　I'll give you these oranges.

Bob :　How about my cat?

Bill :　I can give you two old coins.

Tom :　Be quiet, all of you.

John :　Can I paint now?

Tom :　Each of you can paint a little. John, you can paint now. Bob and Bill, you must wait.

(After a few hours almost every boy in the town has painted for him.)

Tom :　All right. All of you did a good job. Aunt Polly will be here soon, so you'd better go now. Don't stay around here.

(All the boys go away. Tom begins to paint again. Aunt Polly comes up to him.)

Aunt Polly :　What a good boy you are, Tom! The fence looks wonderful. You're almost through, and you did a good job.

Tom:　May I go to the river, Aunt Polly?

Aunt Polly :　Yes, I'll let you go. You've worked enough today. You may go swimming or fishing.

11-3 EXERCISE

A▷ Arrange the sentences.

1. the girl kind is how. ⇨ _____

2. interesting is the story how. ⇨ _____

3. a radio what it small is. ⇨ _____

4. was Helen pretty how. ⇨ _____

5. what flowers has beautiful she. ⇨ _____

6. bad they boys what are. ⇨ _____

B▷ Make sentences. Use the words given.

① watch   ② let

1. _____

2. _____

③ make

3. _____

4. _____

④ hear   ⑤ feel

5. _____

■ **本單元目標**：複習「感官動詞＋原形動詞」的用法，及感嘆句的句型。

■ **在家學習的方法**：家長可多鼓勵孩子將讀書心得記入日記中，如果無法一下子寫成一篇文章，可教他們由造句開始。

THE LOVE LETTER

Once there was a boy who loved a girl very much. The girl's father, however, did not like the boy and did not want their love to grow. The boy wanted to write the girl a love letter, but he was sure that the girl's father would read it first. At last, he wrote this letter to the girl.

> The great love that I have for you
> is gone, and I find my dislike for you
> grows every day. When I see you,
> I do not even like your face;
> the one thing that I want to do is to
> look at other girls. I never wanted to
> marry you. Our last conversation
> was very boring and has not
> made me look forward to seeing you again.
> You think only of yourself.

If we were married, I know that I would find
life very difficult, and I would have no
pleasure in living with you. I have a heart
to give, but it is not something that
I want to give to you. No one is more
foolish and selfish than you, and you are not
able to care for me and help me.
I sincerely want you to understand that
I speak the truth. You will do me a favor
if you think this the end. Do not try
to answer this. Your letters are full of
things that do not interest me. You have no
true love for me. Good-bye! Believe me,
I do not care for you. Please do not think that
I am still your boyfriend.

The girl's father, of course, read the letter first. But he was satisfied that the letter said nothing to show the boy's love.   He was pleased, and then gave the letter to his daughter.

The girl read the letter and was very happy. The boy still loved her !

Do you know why she was pleased ? She and the boy had a secret way of writing to each other. She read the first line of the letter, then the third, then the fifth, and continued reading this way until she came to the end of the letter.

 **LET'S PRACTICE**

Work in pairs.

 A : May I help you?

B : Yes. Can I see that pen, please?

---Useful Expressions---

1. What size is this?
2. Can I try on this dress?
3. Do you have anything larger?
4. I'll take it.
5. I'll take three of these.

2 A : May I help you?

B : Yes, I want two hamburgers and a strawberry milk shake.

A : Yes, sir. Is this to go, or will you eat here?

B : I'll eat here, thank you.

fishburger
orange juice

apple pie
iced tea

hamburger
ice cream cone

Coke
French fries

(Note) : Let students work in pairs and practice these lines.

12-2 SING A SONG

HOME ON THE RANGE

12-3 EXERCISE

Answer the questions.

1. If you were rich, what would you do?

_____

2. If you saw a house on fire, what would you do?

_____

3. If it is sunny tomorrow, what will you do?

_____

4. If you could drive a car, what would you do?

_____

5. If you were a junior high school student, what would you do?

_____

6. If your classmate is sick, what will you do?

_____

7. If you became a monkey, what would you do?

_____

8. If your bicycle were stolen, what would you do?

_____

■ **本單元目標**：複習 if 的句型，包括「與現在事實相反的假設」和「有可能實現的假設」兩種。

■ **在家學習的方法**：如果孩子對此單元不太熟，可將第五冊的第13課拿出來複習，特別要加強習題部分，一定要孩子親自做。

Review 1 > Irregular Verbs

Read after your teacher.

	simple present	simple past	past participle
①	be (am, is / are)	was were	been
②	become	became	become
③	begin	began	begun
④	break	broke	broken
⑤	bring	brought	brought
⑥	build	built	built
⑦	buy	bought	bought
⑧	can	could	—
⑨	catch	caught	caught
⑩	come	came	come
⑪	cut	cut	cut
⑫	do; does	did	done
⑬	draw	drew	drawn
⑭	drink	drank	drunk
⑮	drive	drove	driven
⑯	eat	ate	eaten
⑰	fall	fell	fallen
⑱	find	found	found
⑲	fly	flew	flown
⑳	forget	forgot	forgot; forgotten
㉑	get	got	got; gotten
㉒	give	gave	given
㉓	go	went	gone
㉔	grow	grew	grown
㉕	have; has	had	had
㉖	hear	heard	heard
㉗	keep	kept	kept
㉘	know	knew	known
㉙	leave	left	left

	simple present	simple past	past participle
㉚	lend	lent	lent
㉛	let	let	let
㉜	lose	lost	lost
㉝	make	made	made
㉞	meet	met	met
㉟	put	put	put
㊱	read	read	read
㊲	ride	rode	ridden
㊳	rise	rose	risen
㊴	run	ran	run
㊵	say	said	said
㊶	see	saw	seen
㊷	sell	sold	sold
㊸	send	sent	sent
㊹	shall	should	—
㊺	show	showed	shown; showed
㊻	sing	sang	sung
㊼	sit	sat	sat
㊽	sleep	slept	slept
㊾	speak	spoke	spoken
㊿	spend	spent	spent
(51)	stand	stood	stood
(52)	swim	swam	swum
(53)	take	took	taken
(54)	teach	taught	taught
(55)	tell	told	told
(56)	think	thought	thought
(57)	throw	threw	thrown
(58)	understand	understood	understood
(59)	will	would	—
(60)	write	wrote	written

Review 2 ▷ Tell a Story

Tom Has to Work on Saturday

Note : Since all of your students have performed this play in class, let them tell the story one by one according to these pictures.

Review 3   My School Life

Write a composition.

Name_____ Class_____ No._____

_____

_____

_____

_____

_____

_____

_____

_____

_____

_____

_____

_____

_____

_____

第六冊　學習內容一覽表

單元	內　　容	練　　　習	活　　　動	習　　　作
複習第五冊	1. 我的嗜好 2. 被動式和關係代名詞 3. 一架新的模型飛機 4. 我最好的朋友	Look and read. Make sentences. Look and read. Read and say.		
1	新學年開始	Look and write：讓小朋友練習做簡單的自我介紹，認識班上的新同學。	歌曲：Do your ears hang low？	Write and say.
2	生日禮物	① Look and say：看圖練習用 be going to 來造句。 ② Choose the correct words：選擇正確的過去式動詞。	童詩：Mother Goose.	Fill in the blanks. （複習未來式和過去式）
3	問　路	Find the way：看著地圖幫外國朋友指路。	歌曲：Oh, Susanna！	① Multiple choice. 　（複習數量形容詞） ② Make sentences. 　（複習頻率副詞）
4	蘇珊的筆友	Look and write：練習用英文寫一封信給外國的筆友；再以外國友人的身份回信給台灣的筆友。	遊戲：A secret message.	Fill in the blanks. （複習現在進行式和代名詞的所有格、受格等）
5	我是一隻狗	Who is the strongest？ 演一齣英文話劇：「老鼠嫁女兒」，複習比較級和最高級。	遊戲：Biggest, tallest and fastest.	① Fill in the blanks. ② Read and answer. 　（複習比較級和最高級）
6	蘇珊去紐約	Look and say：請同學上台做小小演說，談談自己的志願。	歌曲：Row, row, row your boat.	Fill in the blanks. （複習附加問句和動名詞）
7	寫日記	Keey your own diary：讓小朋友練習用英文寫日記。	遊戲：An IQ test.	Change sentences. （複習被動式）
8	二個小故事	Look and say：兩人一組，練習看圖一問一答，複習 " How long have you～ " 的句型。	歌曲：Old black Joe	Fill in the blanks. （複習現在完成式）
9	送你的禮物	Look and choose：學習使用英文中的肢體語言、手勢等等。	童詩：Teddy Bear	① Fill in the blanks. ② Make sentences. 　（複習關係代名詞）
10	最後一片葉子（I）	Answer the questions：閱讀課文後，讓小朋友回答問題訓練理解力。	話劇：Tom has to work on Saturday（I）	Answer the questions. （複習連綴動詞）
11	最後一片葉子（II）	Answer the questions：根據課文回答問題，並將讀後心得記入日記中。	話劇：Tom has to work on Saturday（II）	① Rearrange sentences. 　（複習感歎句） ② Make sentences. 　（複習感官動詞和使役動詞）
12	一封情書	Work in pairs：2人一組，練習用英文在商店中購物及速食店中點餐。	歌曲：Home on the range.	① Answer the questions. ② Fill in the blanks. 　（複習與現在事實相反的假設語句）
複習第六冊	1. 不規則動詞三態變化表 2. 看圖說故事 3. 我的學校生活	Read after your teacher. Tom has to work on Saturday. Write a composition.		

學習兒童美語讀本⑥

編　　著／陳怡平

發　行　所／學習出版有限公司　　　☎ (02) 2704-5525

郵　撥　帳　號／05127272　學習出版社帳戶

登　記　證／局版台業 2179 號

印　刷　所／裕強彩色印刷有限公司

台　北　門　市／台北市許昌街 10 號 2 F　　☎ (02) 2331-4060

台灣總經銷／紅螞蟻圖書有限公司　　　☎ (02) 2795-3656

本公司網址　www.learnbook.com.tw

電　子　郵　件　learnbook@learnbook.com.tw

書＋MP3 一片售價：新台幣二百八十元正

2016 年 10 月 1 日新修訂

ISBN 978-957-519-948-7